BUT NOT NATE

Written by
Andrew Gutelle

Illustrated by
Susan Swan

TIME-LIFE FOR CHILDREN
ALEXANDRIA, VIRGINIA

Sunny day?
Hip, hip hooray!
Children rush
outside to play.

But not Nate!

His house is where
he waits *inside*.
He thinks it's fun
to stay and hide.

But not Nate!

Under the fence he tries to wiggle.

Silly Nate! You make me giggle!

Climbing, climbing to the *top*.
In the treehouse they all stop.

No one wants to be the last,
So to the park the kids race *fast*.

But not Nate!
Our little friend is slow, slow, *slow*.
Where is he now? Where did he go?

Puddles of mud the children see.
They step *around* them one, two, three!

**But not Nate!
He went ahead and
squished right *through*!
Oh boy, what fun! May I
squish too?**

The hungry kids want something *hot*,
With ketchup poured on every spot.

But not Nate!
He picked something *cold* as ice.
A tiny taste would sure be nice!

A *small* balloon, a skinny string,
Each kid holds tight to everything.

But not Nate!
His *big* balloon, as you can see,
Is floating up above a tree!

The friends go *down* the slippery slide.
They love to zip and dip and glide.

But not Nate!
Up the ladder,
watch him climb.
Step by step Nate
takes his time!

Hands and shovels dig and scoop,
Full buckets for this busy group.

But not Nate!
There's nothing in his *empty* pail.
Nate has made a sandy trail.

A garden hose? The perfect tool!
Now everybody's *wet* and cool.

But not Nate!
His quiet place is cool and *dry*.
Nate's resting with a butterfly!

**Playtime has come to an *end*.
Gone is each and every friend.**

**But not Nate!
"Let's *begin* again! Let's have more fun!"
Can you help Nate find everyone?**

The kids all laugh and shout "OK!"
No more "nots" for Nate today!